Comeback

Vicki Grant

orca soundings

ORCA BOOK PUBLISHERS

This book is for Jane Buss, who has done so much for me and for so many other Nova Scotian writers.

National Library of Canada Cataloguing in Publication Data:

Grant, Vicki

Comeback / Vicki Grant.

(Orca soundings)

ISBN 978-1-55469-311-5 (bound).--ISBN 978-1-55469-310-8 (pbk.)

I. Title II. Series: Orca soundings.

PS8613.R367C65 2010   jC813'.6   C2009-906838-9

First published in the United States, 2010
Library of Congress Control Number: 2009940841

Summary: When her father disappears, Ria is forced to decide if she really knew him.

Orca Book Publishers gratefully acknowledges the support for its publishing programs provided by the following agencies: the Government of Canada through the Canada Book Fund and the Canada Council for the Arts, and the Province of British Columbia through the BC Arts Council and the Book Publishing Tax Credit.

Cover design by Teresa Bubela
Cover photography by Getty Images

ORCA BOOK PUBLISHERS
PO Box 5626, STN. B
VICTORIA, BC Canada
V8R 6S4

ORCA BOOK PUBLISHERS
PO Box 468
CUSTER, WA USA
98240-0468

www.orcabook.com
Printed and bound in Canada
Printed on 100% PCW recycled paper.
13 12 11 10 • 4 3 2 1

Chapter One

My boyfriend is trying to make me feel better. He's leaning against his locker, one arm over my head, making a little cocoon for me. He tucks a wisp of hair behind my ear and says, "It's not the end of the world, Ria. Who knows? You might even end up liking it. So smile, would you? C'mon. Just a little... Please?"

I appreciate the effort. I really do. Colin's sweet—but it's not helping. He doesn't know how I feel.

How could he?

His life's right off the Disney Channel. The mom. The dad. The three kids. The mischievous but lovable dog. Everyone sitting around the kitchen table, laughing at dumb jokes and flicking corn niblets at each other.

Colin couldn't possibly understand what it's like to live without all that—any more, I guess, than I could have three months ago.

The weird thing is I didn't even know my life was perfect until suddenly it just wasn't anymore. It was like waking up after a car crash and realizing your legs aren't there. Who even thinks about how great walking is before something like that happens?

The word *crippled* pops into my head, and that's enough to get me

started again. I have to close my eyes.

Colin says, "Oh, no. Ria…" I feel the air go out of him.

This isn't fair. I shouldn't make him miserable just because I am. That's the type of thing my mother would do.

What am I saying? That's the type of thing my mother *did* do.

This whole thing is all about *her.* *Her* life, *her* happiness, *her* whatever.

It's as if one morning she just decided she didn't want to be married anymore, and that was that. No explanation. No apology. No nothing.

Next thing we knew, she'd kicked Dad out. She'd fired the housekeeper, cut up our credit cards, took a pathetic little job at an office somewhere and jammed the freezer full of these Styrofoam disks that she insists on calling pizza.

I don't get it. If we're suddenly so poor, why won't she cash the checks Dad keeps leaving for her? He's a big stockbroker. He's got tons of money. He doesn't mind giving it to us. He *wants* to.

Mom's trying to embarrass him. That's what she's doing. She knows it's going to look bad for him to be wining and dining his clients at the best restaurants in town when his own kids can't even "afford" take-out pizza anymore.

I'm sure I sound mad and childish and spoiled—and I probably am—but I can't help it. When this whole thing started, I tried to be supportive. I choked down the frozen pizza. I didn't complain when Mom canceled our trip to Italy. I looked after my little brother Elliot. I even attempted to be sympathetic.

I mean, I'm not totally blind. I can see Dad isn't the easiest guy to be married to. He's away on business too much. He's involved in too many organizations. He's got too many friends, clients, acquaintances, whatever—and they all want to go golfing with him.

I can understand how that would get to Mom.

I figured she just needed a break. After a couple of weeks—and maybe jewelry and a romantic dinner somewhere—she'd remember the good things about Dad, and then we could all just go back to being a family again. That's what I thought.

At least until this morning, when I found out Mom went and sold our house. Now, on top of everything, she's making us move into some gross little condo, miles from all our friends and our schools and—oh, yeah, what a coincidence—our father.

I can't be sympathetic anymore. This is her midlife crisis. We shouldn't all have to suffer from it.

I'm not going to be like that.

I open my eyes and smile at Colin. "I'm fine," I say. "My contacts were just bothering me."

There's no way Colin believes that, but by this point, he's probably had enough of my honesty. He kisses me on the forehead and then starts manhandling me toward the cafeteria. I laugh as if it's all fun and games, but I'm not sure how long I can keep up the act. The thought of having to do my Miss Congeniality thing for the entire lunch-eating population of Citadel High exhausts me.

My phone rings just as we get to the burger lineup. Ms. Meade glares at me and says, "Cell phones. Outside." Normally, I think that rule's totally unfair, but today it strikes me as proof that God just might exist after all. I mumble "Sorry" and slip out the side door onto the parking lot. I can see Colin is torn between keeping an eye on me and placing his order, but he follows me out anyway.

"Hey," I say into the phone.

"Hello, Princess."

"Dad!" I smile for real. I can't remember the last time I did that. "Where are you?"

"Guess."

I don't have to. Colin has already spotted him and is dogging it across the parking lot toward the biggest, shiniest old convertible I've ever seen. It's turquoise and white and has these giant Batmobile fins on the back. Dad's leaning up against it. He's got his tie loosened and his jacket slung over one shoulder as if he's auditioning for *Mad Men*.

I have to laugh. "Where did you get that thing?"

"Thing?! I'll have you know this vehicle once belonged to Elvis Presley."

"Dad."

"Seriously! And Elvis always had a gorgeous redhead in the passenger seat. So hurry up, darlin'. The King's waiting."

By this time, a kid I recognize from my English class has wandered over to check out the car too. Dad gives us the guided tour—the whitewall tires, the original upholstery, the engine, even the ashtrays. I don't know anything about cars, but I can see it's impressing the hell out of the two boys.

Dad basks in the glory for a while, then tosses Colin the keys. "Okay, big guy, let's blow this pop stand."

Colin looks at the keys, looks back at Dad, then yelps like a cowboy. He jumps into the driver's seat.

The other kid starts walking away, but Dad goes, "Whoa. Stop. You too. Get in."

The kid kind of laughs and says, "No. Thanks. That's okay." He tries to slink away, but Dad's not taking no for an answer.

"Life's too short to miss riding in a gen-u-ine mint-condition 1962 LeSabre ragtop." Dad points at the car as if he's sending the kid to the principal's office. "Now hop in, boy! I mean it."

The kid looks at me for help. I shake my head. What can I do? When my father wants something, he gets it.

You can tell the kid's worried there's a hidden camera somewhere, but he shrugs and climbs in the backseat with Dad anyway. I slide in beside Colin. We take off with a screech.

Dad doesn't tell Colin to slow down and doesn't freak out when he comes a tad too close to a parked car. He just reaches over the front seat and cranks up the radio. The wind whips my hair over my mouth and eyes. Colin's hat flies off. People on the sidewalk turn to watch us. We're all hooting and laughing. It's so perfect. It's almost like we're in a commercial.

This whole thing is Classic Dad. The surprise visit at the exact right time.

The amazing car that may or may not have belonged to Elvis Presley. Letting Colin drive. Dragging a stranger along. Turning an ordinary Friday lunch period into something pretty close to a "life moment."

So maybe it's a bit on the flashy side. What's wrong with that? Dad's right. Life is too short not to enjoy it. I'm only seventeen, and I get that. Why doesn't Mom?

I turn around and look at Dad. He's making Tim or Tom—I don't remember the guy's name—sing the doo-wop part of some old rock-and-roll song. The fact that neither of them knows the tune doesn't bother him at all. They're hollering at the top of their lungs like two kids at a campfire.

It's right then that I realize something.

I know how I can fix this thing.

I suddenly know how we can all be happy again.

Chapter Two

It's Dad's face that does it. He's got crow's-feet around his eyes and laugh lines around his mouth that are so dark you'd think they were drawn on with a Sharpie—but it's still a kid's face. There's something twinkly about it. He always looks as if he can hardly wait to find out what's coming next.

Mom's wrinkles go straight down her forehead, right between her eyes. You'd never call them laugh lines. They're from frowning or worrying or trying really hard not to totally lose it.

How did two people that different ever get together?

I look at Dad. He's holding his fist like a microphone and singing, "Ooh, baby, baby, yeah!" The sun makes his eyes look almost as blue as the car. He winks at me, as if I'm the girl he's singing about.

That's when it hits me: Mom and Dad aren't getting back together. The funny thing is, right then, it doesn't even make me sad. It just kind of makes sense. It's like what Colin said. "It's not the end of the world." In fact—it might even turn out to be best for everyone.

All we have to do is tweak the plan a bit.

Instead of Elliot and me moving into Mom's new condo with her, we'll move in with Dad.

Just thinking that makes my mouth stretch into this big lotto-prizewinner grin. I clap my hands over my face. I feel guilty but really, really happy too.

I throw my arms up in the air and let the wind bat them around. It's the perfect solution. Dad can afford us. Mom can't. He loves having us. She's too tired after work to even notice us. We won't have to leave our neighborhood. She can get as far away from it as she wants.

There are a few details that we still have to work out, of course. Dad's apartment is too small for all of us to live there, so we'd have to buy a new place. I'm not much of a housekeeper, so hopefully Manuela isn't mad at Mom for firing her. If she came back to do the cleaning and help with Elliot after school, I could learn how to cook.

I laugh.

Who needs to cook? Dad never says no to going to a restaurant.

In fact, right at this very moment, he's steering Colin toward The Chicken Burger. I'm a little worried that we won't get back in time for the next period, but Dad insists. "What's the matter with you kids? You can't cruise around in a 1962 convertible and not stop for malted milkshakes!"

The Chicken Burger is packed—and everybody, it seems, wants to check out the LeSabre. While Dad chats them up, I reach over and squeeze Colin's hand. He's got gorgeous hands. Athlete's hands. They're big and sinewy, and I love the way the blond hairs stand out against his tan.

I just thought of another thing that makes my new plan so great. Dad has much more liberal ideas about young love than Mom does.

Colin doesn't know that's what I'm thinking, but he can see I'm happy, and that makes him happy too, which makes me even happier. I take a slurp of my milkshake. I don't care that it's got 80,000 empty calories. Everything is different now. Everything is going to be all right.

We get back to school with only minutes to spare before the bell rings. I'm dying to talk to Dad right now about my plan, but there won't be time. That's okay. It can wait until tomorrow. Elliot and I are staying at his place this weekend. We'll work it all out then.

Tim/Tom gives Dad a man hug and heads into class. Colin goes to hand back the keys, but Dad pushes them away.

"I'll make you a deal, Moose. You can keep the car for the weekend if

I can have my little girl alone for a couple of minutes now. Whaddya say?"

Colin has that stunned look on his face again. Dad laughs. "I'll take that as a yes. Now git! Tell your teacher Ria's on her way."

Colin "gits." Dad and I lean against the car and watch him go. Even from behind, you can tell he's grinning his face off. It totally cracks us up.

Dad puts his arm around me. "Listen," he says. "I've got something I need to talk to you about. There's going to be a little change in plans."

For half a second, I wonder if he has the same idea I do. I try not to look too hopeful.

"I won't be able to see you and Elliot this weekend."

"What?" I feel like he just punched me.

Dad pulls his face back in surprise. It's not as if it's the first time he's had to make new arrangements.

"Oh, sorry, sweetie! I have to meet a bunch of investors up north to talk about one of our projects. Believe me, I tried to change it, but it's the only time everyone can get together."

I look away. My breathing has gone shallow and stuttery. I try to act like I'm fine, but I can't. I *need* to see Dad this weekend. I *need* to talk to him about my plan. I suddenly can't stand living with Mom anymore.

"Can I come?" I say. I sound all chipper and fake. Desperation is so embarrassing.

"Aw, honey, you'd hate it. I'm going to some cold little lake in the middle of nowhere. You'd go crazy. There're no shops, no Internet, no cell-phone coverage…"

I know he's making a joke, but I say, "I don't care! Please…please!"

He puts up his hand and says, "Nope. Sorry."

I get this quivery little smile on my face. Dad goes, "Oooh, sweetie pie," as if I'm four and just got a boo-boo on my knee.

"Ria. You *know* I'd take you if I could—but I can't. I've rented a little two-seater plane, and I'm flying it up myself."

"So what's the problem?" I say. "Two seats. One for you. One for me."

He looks at me like I'm missing something obvious. "My point is— I can't fly a plane and clean up your vomit at the same time."

There's nothing I can say to that. He's right. The motion sickness would kill me.

My eyes start filling up with tears, and my smile gets shakier and shakier. I can't believe I'm making such a fool of myself.

Dad squeezes me. "And…," he says.

"And...," he says again, waiting until I pull myself together, "there's another reason you can't go."

I wipe my nose with the tip of my fingers and say in the most mature voice I can, "Oh? What would that be?"

He pulls an envelope out of his pocket. "I've got four tickets for the Chaos of Peace concert this weekend."

I laugh even though there are still tears running down my face. "Dad! How did you get those? They were totally sold out!"

He wags his finger at me. "I never divulge my sources..."

The bell rings. I go to grab the tickets, but he jerks them away. "Ah-ah-ah. Sorry. These come with a couple of strings attached, I'm afraid."

This is so not like Dad it almost scares me. What other crap is going to land on me now?

"One," he says. "No more tears. We Pattersons pick ourselves up, dust ourselves off and get ready for the next party. Okay?"

I nod. As crap goes, that wasn't so bad.

"And the other string?" I say.

"Two of the tickets are for your mom and Elliot."

Is he crazy? Elliot's too young to go the concert, and Mom's too mad. Hasn't he learned? Even just *offering* her the tickets is going to piss her off.

But I don't argue. I'm dying to go to the concert. I say, "Yeah, sure," and try to make it sound like it's a great idea.

Dad isn't falling for that. He looks straight at me for a couple of seconds, then sighs. "She's a good woman, Ria. She just has a lot on her plate at the moment. We've all got to give her a break."

I get up my courage. "Dad, that's what I wanted to talk to you about…"

The second bell rings. I only have a minute. I don't know where to start. I fumble around. "You know… I…well…"

Dad puts his hands on my shoulders. "Hold that thought. You're late already, and Colin's good looks will only distract the teacher for so long. Why don't I book a table for two Monday night at Da Maurizio's, and you can tell me all about it then? Deal?"

Dad and his deals.

"Sure. I'd like that." I'm trying too hard to be brave, and it shows.

He musses up my hair, then gives me a hug. He hugs me so hard, I can hear a little bone in my shoulder squeak.

I head into class. The last I see of him, Dad's got his thumb out and is hitching a ride back to his office.

Chapter Three

I'm in the front row, ten feet from the stage, with my boyfriend on one side and my two best friends on the other. I've got VIP seats, signed CDs and some of the most amazing photos you've ever seen on my iPhone. Helena and Sophie haven't stopped screaming since the band hit their first note. Colin is so pumped, he keeps picking me right up off my feet.

I'm the happiest girl in the world—and I'm laughing at myself.

Seriously.

Yesterday, I'm in the total depths of despair, then Dad gives me concert tickets and *poof!* All my problems disappear.

I'm either easy to please—or really, really shallow.

The music is so loud, I can barely hear it anymore. It probably means I'll be deaf by the time I'm twenty, but at the moment I'm loving it. In a weird way, that much sound is almost like total silence. You can get lost in it.

My mind wanders all over the place. I think about Colin (of course), about the English paper I should have started last week, about how I'm going to decorate my room in the new house, about whether it's normal for the drummer to sweat that much, about a fabulous pair of boots I saw at Project 9 the other day.

Mostly, though, I think about Mom.

For three months, I've been so mad at her. It's as if she wasn't even my mother anymore. She was just bad, mean, inconsiderate, evil.

The truth is, it's *Dad* who should be mad at her. He's the one she kicked out. And yet the only thing he's ever said to me is, "She's a good woman."

Is he really that forgiving—or does he just not know?

I wonder if he'd have said the same thing if he'd seen the look on her face yesterday when I told her about the concert tickets.

You hear about people turning their noses up at something. You think it's just a figure of speech—but Mom actually did it. She actually put her nose up in the air and said, "Oh"—loud clearing of throat—"I'm afraid I'm too busy for that type of thing at the moment."

Then she smiled—or at least made an attempt.

Even with the band playing one of my favorite songs and Colin grooving away beside me, I feel mad all over again. That pitiful attempt at a smile. Why even bother?

If Dad hadn't asked me to cut her some slack, I probably would have yelled at her, but I held back. I knew Helena and Sophie would be thrilled to go to the concert. I wouldn't have to worry about *them* having a good time.

Frankly, Mom saying no to the tickets was a good thing. Why fight with her over it? It was her loss. I could afford to be big about it. That's what Dad would do.

So I just smiled and said, "Oh, too bad." Then I asked her if she wanted me to help her pack. (The sooner she moved, the sooner we could.)

Mom turned and looked at me. I almost didn't recognize her. She'd been so blank in the face ever since Dad left. Right then, though, standing by the sink with a pile of dirty dishes, she almost glowed. It was like seeing light coming out from under a door in a dark hallway. I realized there was a human being in there after all.

She went right back to stacking the dishes. I could tell she was trying not to act too excited about my little offer.

"Well, I'd certainly appreciate the help. Are you sure Colin doesn't have any plans for you this evening?"

"I thought maybe he could help too."

That did it. She leaned against the counter and her face cracked into this huge smile.

Is spending a night with her kids, packing boxes, really Mom's idea of a good time these days?

It's hard not to feel sorry for her.

I bring my mind back to the concert. I look at Colin. His head's cranking away to the music. He doesn't have the best sense of rhythm, and he needs a haircut, but that's why I love him. He doesn't care about that kind of stuff. He just wants to have fun and be happy and make other people happy. (Maybe it really is true that girls always fall in love with someone just like their father.)

Last night, he actually skipped a hockey game to help us pack. He lifted all the heavy stuff for us and got down all the high stuff and lugged all the gross stuff out to the curb so we wouldn't have to soil our delicate hands. He even play-wrestled for ages with Elliot to keep him out of our hair.

We were having a great time until Mom went and said, "It sure is nice to have a man around the house."

She was only joking, but as soon as she said it she realized her mistake.

Her face went blank again. We got all awkward. It was as if the words *Dad* and *Divorce* and *Lonely* and *Sad* were buzzing around our heads, and everyone was too afraid to swat them away.

Colin was the one who did something about it. He reached out and put his hand on Mom's shoulder. It was such a nice thing to do—even if it was the totally wrong thing to do. (I don't think she would have actually cried if he hadn't touched her.)

Luckily, right then, Elliot piped up and said, "Hey! *I'm* a man and *I'm* around the house!"

He was so indignant that we all laughed. Mom turned and squeezed Colin's hand, and I knew she was saying thanks.

The lead singer is clapping his hands over his head, trying to get everyone singing. I stand up and clap too, but my mind is totally on Elliot now. The poor kid is only five. Sometimes I think he doesn't understand what's going on at all. Other times I think he understands too much. I see how hard he tries to remember to put his toys away for Mom and how tight he hangs onto Dad when he comes over to visit. It's enough to break your heart.

Mom's really going to miss him when we go. I'm sorry about that, but it can't be helped. It will be better for Elliot.

I'm going to *make* it better for Elliot.

The crowd starts cheering. I realize the band has left the stage. Colin hustles us out the side exit so we don't get lost in the crush.

We drop the girls off at Sophie's place. Helena's hoarse from screaming, but she manages to croak out, "Tell your father I love him. Seriously. I loved him before he gave us the tickets—but *now I want to marry the guy!*"

Sophie goes, "In-ap-propriate!" She slaps a hand over Helena's mouth, then whispers to me, "Though the truth is, I'm crazy for Steve too. You are *so* lucky!"

We kiss. We hug. We leave. Sophie's right. I am so lucky.

I'm in such a blissed-out state that it takes me a couple of seconds to realize Colin drove right past our street.

"Hey!" I say. "Where you going?"

He gives that one-sided smile of his. It gets me right in my chest.

"There are two places you absolutely have to go when you're driving a 1962 LeSabre. The Chicken Burger. And, of course…"

He turns down the road into Point Pleasant Park.

"…Lover's Lane."

Chapter Four

Colin glides to a stop in front of the seawall. The moon is high and so bright it makes a long white Adidas stripe on the black water.

He lifts one eyebrow and pulls me across the seat toward him. This is all very tempting—I'm a fool for that pine-cone smell of his—but I put both hands on his chest and stop him.

"No," I say. "Next week."

He lifts his face off my neck. "*Next week?*" He looks at me as if I must be joking. "Why?"

I tell him my plan. The move. Hiring Manuela again. Learning to cook. The whole thing. Even the part about Dad and his liberal attitude toward young lovers.

Colin leans against the car door, fiddling with my hair, listening, usually smiling—then he says what I was afraid he was going to say.

"What about your mom? Aren't you worried this will be hard on her?"

I explain all my reasons—the money stuff, how tired she is, how disruptive the move to a new neighborhood would be for Elliot. I'm being as reasonable as I can, but I'm still scared to look at Colin. I can tell by the tilt of his head he's trying to coax me into being nicer than I actually am.

"But it's hard on Dad too," I say. "And remember. He didn't start this. She did."

Colin's quiet for a long time. He plays with my fingers and looks out at the ocean. "It's sad," he says. "They're both such good people. Your mom's so kind and responsible and everything…"

I don't say, *Or at least she used to be.*

"And your father…you'd think someone with all that money would be a jerk or a snob or whatever, but Steve isn't. He's nice. He really wants to help people."

Colin taps his hand on the steering wheel and takes a breath. This must be hard for him to say. "My parents are really grateful for everything he did for us. He changed our lives. If he hadn't invested their savings for them, they'd never have been able to buy their business. They'd never be able to pay for me to go to university next year." He looks me right in the eye. "Your dad's an incredible guy."

Suddenly, this big sob just kind of erupts out of me. It's as if Colin accidentally managed to pinpoint the exact center of my pain. We're both horrified.

Colin groans. "Oh, sorry. Ria. Sorry." He pulls me into his lap and practically cuddles me like a baby. I'm clenching my teeth together and crunching my abs, trying to kill the sobs.

Colin dabs at my face with his shirtsleeve. I can feel his panic.

I push down my chin and swallow. I take a breath. I promised Dad I wouldn't cry anymore. I look at Colin. His face is pleading with me.

"I really love you," I say.

He nods. "Me too." He's almost crying himself.

It's awkward, but I untwist myself from his lap and stretch out on the long front seat. "Come here," I say.

It's after three in the morning when I get home. I'm just praying Mom fell asleep waiting for me. I sneak in the back door and tiptoe across the kitchen.

"Ria?" Mom's just a silhouette in the dark hall.

Damn. She's going to kill me. I check my shirt, make sure the buttons are all done up right. I don't want a scene.

"Sorry, Mom, I…"

She turns on the light. Her skin's so pale, it's almost mauve. She's rubbing her hands as if her knuckles hurt.

"Honey," she says. "You better sit down. I've got some bad news."

Chapter Five

It's as if she's speaking a foreign language. I can't understand her, and it's making me very agitated.

"What are you talking about?"

She just repeats herself. "Your dad sent an sos at about eight o'clock to say he was having mechanical problems. That's all they know. They lost contact with him after that. They believe his plane went down somewhere over Lake Muskeg."

I scream at her in this hoarse whisper. "I know that—but where's Dad? Is he okay?"

Mom looks out the window. It's so dark out, all you can see is her reflection looking back at us.

"They don't know, honey. The rescue team is on its way. They'll know better by morning."

She puts her hand over mine. I'm too stunned and scared to pull it away.

"Why don't you try and get some sleep, Ria? There's nothing we can do now."

Sleep? Who does she think I am? This is my *father*. She might not care about him anymore, but I do. I glare at her until she turns away.

"I'll put the kettle on," she says.

I sit in front of a cold cup of tea and watch the sky go from black to navy to pink to blue.

The phone rings. Mom walks into the hall and stands with her back to me. Her voice is too low to hear. I stare at her, motionless. I feel like a dog waiting for my master to give me a command.

She hangs up and turns toward me. Her lips have gone small, but her eyes are weirdly open.

"Ria. That was Search and Rescue. They have some news."

She sits down next to me and folds her hands on the table. "They found the plane."

That's good. That's good, I think.

"Or what's left of it…It was a very bad crash." She says it slowly so I understand, so I won't ask her any other questions.

"What do you mean?" I say.

I can see her choosing her words. "The plane was destroyed. Just bits and pieces left."

"Did they find him?" I say.

"No."

"He could have got out then! He could be in the woods somewhere! He could have made it to shore…"

"Ria. It was a very bad crash."

"But they didn't *find* him!"

I turn and see Elliot standing in the hall, with his hair all sticking up and his little elephant pajamas on backward. Suddenly, Mom and I are on the same side again. I smile and say, "Morning, sleepyhead!"

Mom hops up from the table and says, "Goodness! Look at the time! I haven't even started your breakfast." She turns on the radio and rummages around for spoons and cereal and bowls.

Elliot sits next to me. He's got a big pout on his face. "Why were you yelling at Mommy?"

Mom bounces over. "Shreddies! Your favorite!"

Elliot takes a mouthful but looks back and forth between the two of us. I realize how sensitive he's become since Dad left. The thought of how much worse this is going to get for him almost kills me.

He says, "I don't like it when you're mean."

Mom says, "Now, now, Elliot. It's not nice to speak with your mouth full." I stick my tongue out at him as if I'm glad he got caught.

Mom says, "And that's not nice either."

We're so busy trying to distract him that neither of us notices the news has come on until we hear, "This hour's headlines. Millionaire stockbroker missing in air crash."

We both leap up. Mom snaps off the radio and says, "Eight o'clock, Elliot! Time to go. Ria, can you help him get dressed so he won't be late for school?"

The kid's not stupid. He knows something's up. I yank him away from the kitchen table with his mouth still full and drag him upstairs. I pretend to be mad at him for crying, but the truth is I'm relieved to have something else to occupy my mind. He doesn't stop whimpering until I buy him a Crispy Crunch on the way to school and let him eat it.

I get this weird thought. Will he hate chocolate bars for the rest of his life because they'll remind him of the day his dad went missing?

The bell rings. Ms. Jordan comes out and takes Elliot by the hand. She doesn't need to tell me that she's heard the news.

Her "Hey, Elliot!" is too cheery, and her voice, when she's talking to me, is too soft. "Call if we can help in any way."

I walk home in a fog. All I can hear is my breathing and my heart beating and this staticky fuzz in my brain. My cell phone rings, but I don't answer it. I don't look at anyone I pass. I just keep walking until I get home.

I push open the door, and for a moment I wonder if I'm in the wrong place. The kitchen is full of people—Aunt Cathy, our next-door neighbors, a couple of guys Dad golfs with, his doctor, his secretary. They all turn and look at me. They all have the same look on their face.

Dread.

They dread having to talk to me.

I'm their worst nightmare.

Chapter Six

These people are all adults. They know they can't just pretend I'm not there. They know they have to say something.

They take a big breath, paste an understanding smile on their faces and, one by one, walk toward me. The women take my hand in both of theirs. The men put an arm around my shoulder. They ask me how I'm doing. (How do they *think* I'm doing? They heard the news.) They say if I need anything— anything at all!—they're only a phone call away. They tell me my dad was a great guy, a fabulous person, a brilliant financial advisor. They go on and on, but this is the only thing I really hear:

Your father *was*.

What's the matter with these people? No one has said he's dead. Not the police. Not the media. There's no body, no witnesses—no proof that he's not lying wet and wounded somewhere, just praying for the sound of the rescue helicopter.

Why have all of his so-called friends given up on him so easily?

I want to scream and push them away, but I don't. I just bite my lip and nod. They give me one last squeeze, then walk away, relieved. They've done their duty.

Colin's the only person to get it right. He plows into the kitchen, out of breath, searching the room for me.

He pushes past the crowd. He hugs me. He says, "I'm here, Ria." For some reason, that's what actually makes me cry. He says, "I'm not going anywhere," and that makes me cry even more. He just sits there hugging me until I stop.

I feel like a celebrity with my own bodyguard. People still look at me, still smile, but with Colin there, hardly anybody gets up the nerve to say anything to me. I feel calmer. There's still that crazy thudding in my chest, but it's bearable.

Ms. van de Wetering arrives from school with a big tray of muffins. (I didn't realize Dad managed her money too.) She brings one over on a plate and tells me to eat it.

She doesn't get all soppy on me, thank god. She just says, "This is tough, Ria. Make sure you get enough sleep. And don't worry about school. I'll get your teachers to email your assignments or send them home with Colin...If I were as slim as you, I'd have some jam with that. You want some?"

I shake my head. She mumbles something to Colin about letting him off the hook for class today too, then gives me a matter-of-fact pat on the shoulder. "Chin up, kiddo."

And I do keep my chin up—at least until the door bangs open and Sophie and Helena fly in. They throw themselves on me, sobbing. Tears and mascara are streaming down their faces. Everybody turns to look.

Helena keeps going, "It's not fair! It's not fair! Why Steve?" Sophie takes my face and forces me to look at her. "Ria. We loved him too. We all did. You know that."

I start to shake. They hold me closer. They think they've touched me with their heartfelt tears, but that's not it. What's getting me is realizing that this is just another drama for them. They'll make their big public display of grief, and then they'll go home and text their friends with the latest scoop. *OMG. Did you hear about Ria's dad?*

I push them away. "Sorry," I say. "Sorry. I got to get some air."

I head toward the back door. Mom's there, thanking Helena's grandmother for the casserole. She turns to me with that blank look on her face. Everyone else probably thinks she's broken-hearted about the accident—but I know different. She's had the same look on her face for months now. The fact that Dad is missing hasn't changed a thing for her.

I can't stand it.

I turn and head for the front door instead. Helena starts running after me.

I put my hand up. I only manage to squeak out, "No. No. Please."

I step out onto the front deck. The sun is shining, and it's warmer than it's been in days. I think of Dad, in the woods somewhere, in pain—and I'm at least thankful for the weather. He won't be cold. The helicopters will be able to find him. He'll make it. He'll come back.

I'm not sure exactly how to pray, so I just whisper, "Please. Please. Please."

I hear a car pull up in front of the house. I open my eyes. I see Tim/Tom get out the passenger door. He's carrying a bouquet of flowers—bright blue carnations wrapped in a green paper cone.

I'm surprised—he doesn't seem the flower type. Then I notice all the other bouquets and cards and candles and balloons piled up against our front fence. It's like a shrine.

Or a grave site.

My teeth start chattering.

Tim/Tom says, "Sorry for your loss," then nips back into his car before I can say thanks or scream at him.

Chapter Seven

Colin must sense there's something wrong. In a flash, he's out the door with his hands on my waist, whispering in my ear. "It's okay, Ria. It's okay. We're getting out of here."

I don't ask where. I can't. I just let him take me down the stairs, put me in the LeSabre and drive. It's as if someone slipped a drug into my food.

I'm not connected to my body anymore. I'm floating off to the side somewhere.

We're sitting at an intersection waiting for the lights to change when I get knocked back to reality. There's a woman I recognize in the next lane. She's looking at me. I suddenly see myself as she sees me: out cruising with my boyfriend in my flashy turquoise convertible. It's almost as if there's a thought bubble over her head reading, *How heartless can that girl be? Her father could be dead!*

The light turns green, and I blurt out, "Go! Go!" It startles Colin. He turns and sees the lady in the next car too. I don't know if he understands or not, but he hits the gas.

He keeps one hand on my leg, the other on the wheel. He drives straight to Point Pleasant Park. "It'll be quiet here," he says.

He parks the car and leads me up a winding trail through the woods to an old tumbledown army fort. In the summer, there'd be bus tours and day camps and people getting their wedding photos taken here, but today there's no one except the occasional power walker.

Colin drags a picnic table over so that it's half-hidden by one of the old stone walls.

We lay side by side on the tabletop. This stray thought floats in from my previous life: I should have some sunscreen on. I'm the type that burns.

So's Dad. Is he wet and wounded and now sunburned as well?

Am I weird even wondering that?

I reach over and take Colin's hand. At least here, I don't have to worry what other people think. I say, "Thank you for rescuing me."

He turns to me and smiles. He's got one eye squinted up from the sun. The other eye is as green as a Granny Smith apple. "Thank you, nothing," he says. "I just wanted you to myself."

It's such a Dad thing to say— one of those fibs he comes up with just to make you feel good. I do my best to play along.

"You're lying," I say. "You would have been happy to stay there all day— or at least until the muffins ran out."

We both laugh even though it's not that funny.

"I just couldn't stand it," I say. "Everybody looking at me. Everybody expecting me to act a certain way. Even Helena and Sophie doing their big drama-queen thing. It made me want to scream."

I get up on one elbow and look at Colin. "He's not dead," I say. "I know it. How am I supposed to take everybody's stupid condolences when he's not even dead? It makes me so mad."

Colin gets up on one elbow too. He puts his hand on my hip. "People are just trying to be nice, Ria."

I squish my eyes together and let out this sort of frustrated growl. "Well, they aren't nice. They're making me feel terrible. And I. Can't. Handle. It."

I flop back down on the tabletop with my arm over my face. We're quiet for a long time.

"Fine," Colin says. "You don't have to handle it."

He leans over me. "Forget about other people. We don't have to spend time with them. I'll pick you up when I get out of school, and we'll go somewhere, just you and me. We can act however we like. We can do whatever we want. We can be sad or happy or mad—whatever we feel like. Okay?"

I don't know what I'd do without him.

Chapter Eight

I stay home and sleep or watch movies
or pretend to read a book until three in
the afternoon, when Colin comes over.
We pick Elliot up from school, eat
a quick meal, then disappear.

Disappearing—that's what this is
all about. Colin put the roof up on the
LeSabre. It still attracts attention, but
most people don't notice me curled up

in the passenger seat now.

We drive to the park. On warm nights, we sit up by the fort. On colder nights, we find an out-of-the-way parking spot and stay bundled up in the car.

Despite what that might sound like, these aren't just giant make-out sessions. Sometimes we watch a movie on my laptop. Sometimes we turn on the inside light and do our homework or play Mankalah. Once, Colin put on an oldie radio station and we slow-danced under the streetlamp.

Other times—like at least once a day—I just sit in the front seat and cry.

Tonight, I cry more than usual. It's been five days since the accident. Divers have only found one of Dad's boots and the sleeve of his jacket. Crews have searched the surrounding forest. There's no sign of him.

They're very sorry, the man in charge said today, but they've called off the rescue mission. The best they can hope for now is to recover the body.

Steve Patterson is officially presumed dead.

"Presumed!" I want to scream. "How can they presume? They don't know Dad. They don't know what he's capable of. It's only been five days."

I bawl my eyes out. Colin just keeps passing me Kleenex. I don't know how he isn't completely grossed out. My eyes are red, my nose is huge, and my forehead is throbbing as if I've got some big pumping heart in there instead of a brain.

When I've finally exhausted myself, Colin takes my hand. He says, "Ria. I know this is hard, but I think you're going to have to accept that your dad is gone."

I try to pull away, but he won't let me.

"That lake is really deep and really cold. The plane was completely destroyed. Even a guy as smart and athletic and tough as Steve couldn't have survived that."

I glare at him, but he won't stop, he won't let me go.

"I bet your dad's looking down on us right now and wishing he could have stuck around for a whole lot longer. But I also bet that he wouldn't want you to be getting bloodshot eyes over him."

As if I have a choice! I turn away.

"He'd want you to pick yourself up, pull yourself together. He wouldn't want you to miss out on life just because he wasn't around anymore. He'd be telling you to live large. Go for it. Seize the day. That's the kind of guy he was. Am I right?"

He lifts my chin. "Go big or go home! Party hearty. Eat, drink and be merry."

He just keeps talking until I break down and laugh.

He *is* right. Those are exactly the types of things Dad would say.

I wipe my face and put on the Patterson smile.

"So I'd like to make a suggestion…" Colin leans over into the backseat and pulls out two champagne flutes and a bottle of Lime Rickey. That makes me really laugh. Only Colin would remember that Dad loved Lime Rickey.

He fills up our glasses. The street-lamp makes the green of the pop look radioactive.

"From now on, when you think of your dad, I want you to remember all the people he made happy, all the people he made laugh, and all the people, of course, he made rich. I'll certainly be thinking of him next year when I head off to university with my tuition paid."

We clink glasses.

Colin says, "To Steven John Patterson. I just hope that some day I'll be half the man he was!"

I think he already is.

Chapter Nine

It's easy to feel happy when I'm with Colin. It's a lot harder when he's not around.

I know I should go back to school, but the thought of everyone looking at me with those sad faces is more than I can stand.

Instead, for the last couple of days, I've just hung out at home in my sweatpants and glasses, waiting for Colin to show up. Food nauseates me. Movies bore me, and TV depresses me. Exercise is beyond me. Mostly I just sit and "read." I've been on page 27 for three days now.

I throw my book across the room.

I'm ashamed of myself. Dad didn't raise me to be some helpless damsel who just waits around to get rescued.

I stand up straight and take a big breath. I'm going to start working on some of those assignments Ms. van de Wetering has been sending home. Tomorrow I go back to class.

I sit at the kitchen counter and turn on my laptop. A math test Tuesday. A chemistry lab that I'll have to borrow somebody's notes for. A 500-word essay for Global Affairs: *Using printed and online sources, explain how China's growing economy is impacting our global environment.*

Okay. I can do that.

I remember a TV documentary about water pollution in China. This sudden image of Dad's plane slamming into the water flashes in my brain, but I shake it away.

I'm a Patterson. Up and at it.

I google *China, environmental impact*. I scroll down. I don't see what I'm looking for, but after a while I notice something. I'm feeling good. For the first time since Dad went missing, I'm me again. Just a seventeen-year-old girl, cramming to get her homework done. It's comforting.

I find a listing for the documentary, or at least one like it.

I click, and a website opens for an all-news station. The link to the documentary is on the left. I should just open it, but I don't. I scan the news headlines instead. I realize I've been in a bubble since the accident. I hadn't heard anything about the earthquake in Central America or the scandal over the Best Actress Oscar or the psycho in Montreal who hijacked a bus full of tourists.

I also hadn't heard the news about my father.

Millionaire's Death Suspected Suicide

In life, Steve Patterson projected the perfect glossy image of the self-made man—brilliant, charming, athletic, generous. Rising from an impoverished childhood, he became the darling of the investment industry, often earning 20 and 30 percent returns for his clients, even during recessions.

Now, eight days after his presumed death in a plane crash, a different picture is emerging. Reports are beginning to stream in of investors finding their bank accounts drained and their financial portfolios worthless. Mr. Patterson *may have defrauded his clients of up to $100 million.*

Shaken employees at S.J. Patterson Financial Holdings have been unwilling to respond to reporters' questions.

Police now suspect that Saturday's plane crash was not accidental. "Suicide is definitely one of the motives we're pursuing," said Sergeant Jo Yuen. "Our preliminary investigation suggests Mr. Patterson was aware that authorities were closing in on him. He must have known that financial ruin was all but certain for both him and his clients."

The Halifax Hospital, the Steamfitter's Union and Chebucto Community College are just some of the major institutions likely to have lost millions through their investments with S.J. Patterson Ltd.

Sadder, though, is the fate of the countless smaller investors—the pensioners and independent business owners—for whom Mr. Patterson had once been a hero.

Chapter Ten

No. No. No. No. That's all I can think. This is wrong. It's a mistake. It has to be.

I'm trembling like an old man. I google *S.J. Patterson*. *The Herald*, *The Times*, *Newsnet*—they're all running the same story.

Somebody—some sad, bitter, twisted little person who was jealous of Dad's success or couldn't stand how popular he was or who hated him for some other petty reason—made up a lie, and now everybody believes it.

I've got to do something. I've got to stop it.

I think of our Media Arts teacher talking to us about net safety. Warning us how writing one stupid thing, posting one "inappropriate" photo could haunt you for the rest of your life.

I can't stop it. I'll never be able to stop it.

I hear Mom moving around upstairs, and some younger part of me wants to run to her, crying. I know right away, though, that she won't help me. She doesn't love Dad anymore. She'd no doubt be happy to finally have an excuse for kicking him out.

I squeegee the tears off my face with my hands and force my lips to stay still. I've got to figure out what to do. Call the media? Talk to a lawyer? What good would that do? I'm a kid. I'm *his* kid. Who's going to listen to me?

I do the only thing I can think of. I call Colin.

His phone's off.

Of course. "No cell phones on school property."

I'm suddenly afraid that Mom's going to come down the stairs and find me like this.

I've got to get out of here. I'll go to school. I check the time. Colin will be in French. He'll know what to do.

I go into the bathroom and splash water on my face. I look terrible. My skin's the color of raw bacon.

I can't go out like this. Dad would never go out like this. "Put on your game face and your best shirt." That's what he always says.

I hide my grungy T-shirt under the Club Monaco coat I bought just before everything happened. I brush my hair into a ponytail. Rub on some concealer, mascara and lip-gloss. I should put my contacts in too, but there's only so much my eyes can take.

Luckily, Colin left the LeSabre here last night. I grab the keys and scream up the stairs, "I'm going to school. Can you pick up Elliot?" I slip out the door before Mom can ask why.

The pile of flowers and cards on our front lawn has tripled since Sunday. It made me mad the first time I saw it, but not anymore. Now it's proof those stories are all garbage. Look, everyone! See how much people love Steve Patterson!

I run down the steps to take a closer look. Yellow roses from someone named Stacy. A card "from your favorite baristas!" A candle from Mrs. Purcell across the street. And a cardboard sign written in bright red letters—*Burn in hell, you scumbag.*

I almost lose my balance. I scrunch the sign up and stuff it into my purse. I see another card. *Gone but not forgotten—just like my money. Some day you'll pay.* I grab that too, as well as the bouquet of flowers with the obscene note attached.

I should go through everything, get rid of all this stuff. What if Elliot sees it? I picture him asking me what the sign says.

A white van with a satellite dish on top turns onto our street. It's a TV crew, the *Live at Five!* mobile unit.

I'm breathing way too fast. What should I do? Stay and defend Dad? How? What would I say?

I pretend I'm a stranger just stopping to look at the flowers. I get in the LeSabre and drive away. I've never driven such a big car before. It's just one more thing I can barely handle.

Mrs. Lawrence, the school secretary, looks at me funny when I walk in the door. "Ria. I didn't expect to see you back, considering, um…"

Considering what? We're both paralyzed for a second. We both know what she meant to say. She goes pale and starts rummaging around in her drawers in a desperate attempt to look busy. I use it as an excuse to go.

I feel her eyes follow me down the hall. I feel Mr. Samson's eyes follow me too. And the three girls I pass by at the water fountain. And the kids in the gym class, heading out to the field. Everybody's looking at me.

Do they see the girl whose father went missing?

Or the girl whose father is a scumbag?

Chapter Eleven

I knock at room 208. Mrs. LeBlanc answers the door. "Oui?"

I lean forward and whisper, "Sorry—but I need to speak with Colin MacPherson."

Students aren't supposed to interrupt classes, but Mrs. LeBlanc knows who I am. She gives me a sympathy smile—

the type I've been dreading—and says, "One moment…"

She pushes the door open. "Colin M. You have a visitor…"

The whole class turns and looks at me. Some of them put their hands over their mouths and whisper. I feel like one of those prisoners they used to chain up in the public square.

Colin has a strange look on his face. He must know how upset I am. He fumbles with stuff on his desk for a second, and then he gets up and starts walking toward me. He's halfway across the room when Jared Luongo screams out, "Hey, Ria. Looks like your dad finally got what he deserved!"

There's a moment of confusion when everyone gasps and chairs screech and Mrs. LeBlanc tries to restore some kind of order.

I don't know what I expect Colin to do. Pound the guy? Run to me? Murmur something soothing in my ear like, "Don't listen to him. He's a jerk"?

I don't know what I expect—but anything would have been better than what he does.

He hesitates.

"Colin?" I'm so shocked I can barely make the word come out.

He takes three steps toward me and stops, just out of arm's length.

He opens his mouth to say something, but he doesn't have to.

I know immediately that he's heard the stories. That he's believed them. That he's chosen them over me.

I stand there with my mouth open, my eyes desperately scanning the room for another explanation. That's when I see Helena. I forgot she's in this class. I feel a little twitter of hope—but she picks up her pen and starts writing in her notebook.

She can't even look at me.

I turn and race down the hall. A door opens, and Mr. Goldfarb says, "No running in the…" He sees it's me and slips back into his classroom.

He knows too.

Everybody knows.

I keep running until I get to the LeSabre.

The whole way home, all I can think about is Colin. I can't believe he'd do this to me—do this to Dad! I feel so betrayed and hurt and angry—but then it's as if some acid trickles into my brain. I see the words *multimillion-dollar scam*, and just for a second I imagine the MacPhersons losing everything they own because of something my father did.

I feel like I'm in a horror movie and there's some maniac waiting for me behind every door.

I just want to get home—whatever that means. I push my foot to the floor and gun it.

I haven't even turned onto our street, and already I see at least four media vans camped outside our house. I can't face them. I take a hard turn to the left and park the next street over. I sit there stunned for at least an hour, too scared to move. Kids are going to be coming home from school soon. They're going to look at the car. They'll look at me. I get out and sneak home the back way, through a neighbor's yard. The neighbor sees me from her dining room window and waves.

I wave back. She obviously doesn't believe the stories.

Or she hasn't heard them yet.

Mom is sitting with Elliot at the kitchen table while he eats his after-school snack. She stands up when I walk in the door. It's weirdly formal. It's scary.

She says, "Ria, I'm glad you're back," but she doesn't look glad at all.

"There's something I need to talk to you and Elliot about." She sits down and pats the chair so that I'll sit down too.

I don't like the sound of this. She's going to say something about Dad. I can tell. I want to yell at her—I *would* yell at her—but Elliot is here, looking so cute and innocent and almost happy, eating his oatmeal cookie.

I hold my purse in my lap as if I'm ready to bolt at any moment.

"You may have noticed the vans outside," she says.

"Yes!" shouts Elliot. This is a major event for him. "*Live at Five!* Just like on TV. I can hardly wait to tell my teacher!"

Mom reaches out and ruffles his hair. "Hmm. Honey, I don't know if that's such a good idea."

That confuses Elliot. His teacher loves *Live at Five!*

75

"Why?" he says.

Mom ignores him. He holds his cookie so tightly, a big piece breaks off, and he doesn't even pick it up.

Mom's lips smile. "In many ways, your father was a wonderful man... He certainly loved you both very, very much."

I know it's coming.

"But there are some things about him you should probably know." She clears her throat. "He was a stockbroker. That means that people gave him their money to invest for them."

Elliot's eyes are huge. He's trying really hard to be good, to understand.

"What does 'invest' mean?"

She explains it to him. I know I only have a minute. She'll tell him what "invest" means, and then she'll tell him what "multimillion-dollar scam" means.

She's going to tell Elliot our father is a criminal. I know she is. That's what she wants. She'll turn his own son against him. There will be no one but me to believe Dad anymore.

"Daddy buys companies for people?" Elliot says. "I don't get it."

Mom looks away, trying to come up with another way to explain the stock market to a five-year-old.

"Excuse me," I say. "I know this is important—but could we talk about it later? Colin wants to take Elliot and me rock climbing at the Great Wall this afternoon."

Elliot starts bouncing up and down in his seat. "Yeah! Yeah! We're going to the climbing wall!"

Mom doesn't know what to do. I can see that. Her little talk isn't going as well as she planned, and there's no way Elliot will be in any state to listen now.

She sighs. She rubs both hands over her elbows and says, "When will you be back?"

"He wanted to take us out for burgers too"—more squeals of delight from Elliot—"so I doubt we'll be home before eight, eight thirty."

Mom knows when she's beat.

"Okay, Elliot. But you've got to take your medicine before you can go."

Normally, Elliot hates using his asthma puffer, but this time he practically swallows it. I don't waste any time stuffing him into his shoes and sweater. We're out the door in three minutes.

Elliot thinks we're scrambling over the back fence because we're practicing for the climbing wall.

Chapter Twelve

I'm not scared anymore.

No. That's wrong. I *am* scared, but
I barely notice it now. It's like a noise
that bothers you for a while, but then
you get used to it and almost don't hear
it anymore.

Elliot's strapped in the front seat of
the LeSabre, babbling away as if we're
going to a birthday party. I realize that

sooner or later I'm going to have to tell him what's up.

I hear the sound of scared again.

We're heading out of town. We pass the turnoff to Colin's street.

"Hey!" Elliot goes. "Aren't we picking Colin up?"

"Ah, no, not right now." He turns and looks at me with one eye closed. It's his angry pirate face.

"Why not?"

"Sorry, Elliot. Can't talk now. Got to figure out where I'm going."

That much at least is true. Where *am* I going?

I don't know. I've just got to get out of here.

I've got to go someplace where nobody knows us. Somewhere we can ride this thing out.

I'll get a job. I'll put Elliot in school. We'll be okay—better than we are here, that's for sure. I'll look after him.

I'll bring him up to be just like Dad—
good and smart and funny and kind.

Some day when this mess is cleared
up, the two of us will sue all the people
who said bad things about our father.
Then we'll be rich again. We'll have the
last laugh.

I press too hard on the gas. I don't
mean to. All of a sudden, I'm excited.

Dad always said, "Crisis is just
another word for opportunity."

I take the ramp onto the highway
and break out into a smile.

I can do this.

I wish I knew how to put the top
down. I have this urge to just gun it,
feel the wind in my hair. It seems like
the appropriate thing to do. This should
be a celebration, not some sneaky
little escape. We have nothing to be
ashamed of.

We'll get our own little apartment,
Elliot and I. I'll decorate it. I'll learn

to cook. I'll throw him a big birthday party when he turns six and invite all his new friends.

"Ria. We're going the wrong way to the Great Wall." Elliot's neck is stretched out so he can see over the dashboard.

I consider saying, "No, we aren't," and stringing him along for a while, but I don't. I think of all those lies about Dad and how much they hurt, and I realize I've got to tell the truth. I promise myself that I'll always tell Elliot the truth.

"You're right, sweetie. This isn't the way to the Great Wall. We're actually going somewhere else."

Elliot's eyes are wide open, and his bottom lip is rolled down. "Where?" he says in a tiny little voice.

"On an adventure!" I sound like I'm hosting a preschool program. "Mommy can't look after us anymore, so we're going to get a new home somewhere else…" I want him to throw his hands up in the air and go "Yeah!" like he did before, but he doesn't. He looks at me as if I'm the worst liar ever. Then he bursts into tears.

"I don't like adventures! I want Mommy!" He kicks the dashboard and throws his head back and forth as if someone is slapping his face.

I feel like I pulled the wrong stick out of the Jenga tower. All my plans crash to the ground. I'm going "Shh! Shh! Elliot. Calm down!" but I'm having trouble even calming myself down.

Why did I think this was going to be easy?

There's an exit coming up. I could turn around there and be home by six. I could turn around, take Elliot to the Great Wall and be home by eight.

I put on the blinker—but I drive right past the exit.

I can't go home to Mom and the lies and the fact that Colin isn't there anymore.

Elliot is howling and thrashing away. I worry his shoes are going to leave scuff marks on the white leather upholstery.

I do my best to blank him out and lean into the windshield. I tell myself to keep going. I'll figure something out.

Elliot's crying eventually winds down into a wheezy sort of whimpering. He stops asking me where we're going. The sky starts getting dark, and my hands go numb from clenching the steering wheel.

I notice the gas is almost on empty. I pull off at the next exit and look for a service station. The whole time, my head is frantically making new calculations. How far can we get before Mom sounds the alarm? How far can we get on a tank of gas? How far can we get before Elliot melts down?

I pull up to the pump and get out my wallet. It sounds stupid, but this is the first time I realize I actually have to find a way to pay for everything.

Mom cut up my credit card. I've got $18 in bills, maybe a couple bucks more in change. I have a debit card, but I doubt there's more than $35 in my account.

I get a little electric shock of panic, but then I think, *No. Something will come up. We'll be okay.* That was always Dad's attitude.

I start filling the tank. I can't believe how little time it takes to hit $30. I tell Elliot not to move, and I go into the station to pay. The girl at the counter swipes my card. I key in my PIN and hold my breath. It goes through. That's a good sign.

I get out some change and buy a Coke and a bag of chips for Elliot. I immediately feel guilty. Mom would never let him eat like that.

At least the junk food makes Elliot happy for a while. I turn the radio on to the corniest station I can find. For an hour or so, we cruise along the highway with the music blasting. If I could just forget all the other stuff, it would almost seem like we're on an adventure.

I'm starting to pass signs for places I've only ever heard of on the weather report. I switch off the radio when the eight o'clock news comes on. It dawns on me I won't always be able to just turn things off. Someday, Elliot will hear the stories. I'll have to be ready.

The sky is black now—blacker than it ever gets in the city. I imagine our house all lit up by the television lights. Mom is no doubt starting to listen for the sound of Elliot and me coming up the stairs.

How long before she gets worried? How long before she calls? I reach into my purse and turn off my cell. I don't want Elliot asking why I'm not answering my phone.

"I need to pee, Ria."

I don't want to stop yet. I want to get as far away as I can.

"Can you wait?" I say.

He doesn't have to answer. I can tell by the way he's fidgeting that I've got to find a washroom fast.

What if he doesn't make it? What if he wets his pants? I should have packed him a change of clothes.

I take the next exit and, thankfully, there's a service station just a minute down the road. I look at the gas gauge. We're practically on empty again. This car is going to bankrupt me.

Elliot runs into the washroom, holding his crotch.

A guy in his twenties watches him run in and laughs. "Been there, done that," he says. He notices the LeSabre. "Nice car."

I nod. I'm too worried about money to answer. We have to eat, find a place to sleep…

"How does it drive?"

"Good," I say and shrug. I'm trying to brush him off, but then suddenly I get an idea. "Want to give it a spin?"

He looks at me like, *Are you kidding?* and says, "Yeah!"

"Okay," I say. "Twenty bucks for twenty minutes."

I can see the guy's surprised that I'd actually charge him, but it doesn't stop him.

"Sure." He hands me a twenty. "And here, take my birth certificate too. Don't want you worrying about me taking off on you."

Elliot comes out of the washroom just in time to see the guy get in our car.

He doesn't ask why. I think he's scared of answers now.

I hold his hand and watch the car pull out onto the road. There's a bunch of people standing in front of the gas station, and they all watch too. You sure can't hide in a 1962 LeSabre.

Elliot and I have been sitting on the curb waiting for about ten minutes when a bus pulls up. The people in front of the station all pile on. It dawns on me that no one pays much attention to a bus.

I hear a little *ding* in my brain.

"C'mon, Elliot!" I say. "Want to go for a ride?"

The sign on the bus says *Cypress-Riverview*. The driver is standing outside, having a smoke, while the passengers get settled in their seats.

I've got $20 in my hand from the guy. Roughly eighteen more in my wallet. Who knows how much—if anything— in my account. I'll need to save some for food. That means I could spend about $30 on bus tickets.

"Excuse me," I say. "How much does it cost to go to"—I check the window for the name again—"Cypress?"

The driver grinds his cigarette out with his foot.

"Cypress? Twenty-eight bucks."

My shoulders sink. This isn't going to work.

"That's for you. If your son is six or under, he travels free."

Elliot says "I'm not her son" as if the driver just accused him of being an ax murderer.

I said, "I'll take two."

I leave the guy's birth certificate at the convenience store. I don't know what he's going to think when he comes back, but I have nothing to be ashamed off. Twenty bucks isn't bad for a mint-condition LeSabre.

Chapter Thirteen

It's after midnight when the bus pulls into Cypress. It's a tiny little town, not the type of place you could get lost in, that's for sure.

Elliot is sound asleep. I should carry him, but I'm too tired. I wake him up as gently as I can. He's sweaty and confused, but he doesn't complain. He staggers off the bus like a little pint-sized drunk. Any other time in my life, I probably would have laughed, but nothing's very funny at the moment.

What are we going to do now?

I look at the benches in the bus station and I'm tempted just to crash there, but that's not going to work. Mom will have called the police by now. We'd be found in no time.

I've got about $10 left. We can't get a hotel for that kind of money, and we'll freeze if we stay outside.

Who cares? This is hopeless. Why did I even think I could get away with it? Those are the kind of thoughts going through my head. I sit down on a bench and put Elliot on my lap. We'll just wait here until the police come and get us.

There's a noise. I look up and see a man walk out a door marked *Lost and Found*.

Just like us, I think. Lost and found. Thinking that makes me feel smart, as if I was the only person in English class to identify the theme of the novel.

But then that Patterson part of me kicks in.

No. We aren't lost, and we don't want to be found.

We left on purpose. To make a better life for ourselves. This is what we want to do.

I jump up and run over to the door, dragging Elliot with me.

"Phew!" I say. "I'm so glad we weren't too late to catch you."

The guy locks the door. "Well, actually you are, dear. It's twelve thirty and I'm going home."

"Oh, please!" I say. "I left a bunch of stuff on the bus last week and I really, really need it!" The tears in my eyes aren't just for show—but they work.

The guy rubs his hand over his mouth, sighs and opens the door.

"What did you lose?" He says it as if I'm always asking him to help me.

"Um…a blanket, a hoodie, a sweater…" I'm trying to think of what else we might need.

The guy holds up a hand. "Whoa. Okay, let's start there. What color blanket?"

"What color?" I say. I realize I've got to guess the right color or I'm not going to get the blanket. It's like some cruel game show. "Ah…gray," I say.

The guy puts his fist on his hip and sizes us up. Elliot, shivering in his little sweater, me in my skinny rumpled jacket. It sure doesn't look like a $200 Club Monaco trench anymore.

"Right," he says. "Wait here."

He comes back with his arms full of stuff: a red polar fleece blanket, sweatpants and a U of T hoodie for me, a Superman tracksuit and parka for Elliot.

"Do these look like yours?" he says. He's just playing along.

Elliot says, "A Superman suit! Can I have it?"

The guy has a sort of Santa Claus laugh. "Yup. As long as you catch some bad guys for me."

"Thanks," I say. "Thank you so much."

The guy shrugs and locks up again. "No problem. You take care of yourself now."

I make Elliot change in the women's washroom with me. He's got a lot more pep since he snagged the Superman suit. I stuff our old clothes into my purse, and we step out into the cold.

It's a beautiful night. The stars are as sharp and white as LED lights against the black sky. I don't know what I was thinking. This isn't the type of night to give up.

Chapter Fourteen

This is going to sound really out there, but I'll say it anyway.

It's as if Dad is here with us. Not in the flesh. Not walking along the deserted road with us. I don't mean that. (I'm not totally losing my mind.) Just sort of here in my head. It's almost like having a motivational speaker playing on my iPod, telling me to keep going, keep positive, keep the faith. We'll be all right.

I'm exhausted, but I don't stop. I just keep walking—and talking. The least I can do is make it fun for Elliot. I tell him all the old stories I can remember from our camping trips with Dad. When I run out, I make up some new ones. It keeps Elliot moving. We walk for a good hour or so. We trudge along past little brick office buildings and old wooden houses and the odd convenience store. I don't know where we are exactly, but I can see we're coming to the edge of town. The buildings are thinning out. There's a highway in the distance.

Elliot's barely able to walk upright anymore. His weight is pulling at my shoulder socket. I don't let it bother me. I tell myself it feels just like a good yoga stretch.

We come to a small park. Elliot sees a bench and plunks himself down before I can stop him. "I need to go to sleep, Ria."

He's right.

I know I can't take him any farther— but he can't pass out here. If the cops see two kids sleeping on a park bench, they'd pick us up even if they didn't know we were missing.

"That's a terrible bed!" I say and pull Elliot back up onto his feet. I pretend I don't notice the whimpering. "Want to see a better one?"

I have no idea what I'm going to show him. I drag him around the park searching for a hiding spot to lie down.

I notice a big old pine tree with branches that go right to the ground.

"Look! A teepee!" I say it like it's the most exciting thing in the world, but Elliot couldn't care less. He's so tired, he's swaying around like a Fisher Price Wobble Penguin.

I pull back the branches, and we crawl underneath.

It's surprisingly roomy in here. Plenty of space for us to curl up in. I feel better right away. It seems so safe and cozy. There's something about the smell, too, that's nice.

At first, I think that's because it reminds me of Christmas, but then my heart thuds and I know that's wrong.

I'm not smelling Christmas.

I'm smelling Colin and that pine soap he uses. I suck back a big gulp of air and even still, I feel like I'm not getting enough oxygen.

Elliot says, "Ria?" and I can tell I've scared him. I shake Colin out of my head. He was from my old life. This is a new one.

"Remember Dad showing us how to make a mattress in the woods?" I say. "Should we make one now?"

Elliot helps me sweep the pine needles into a pile. I put my purse on the ground for a pillow. I spread the blanket over the needles.

"Crawl in," I say to Elliot.

He lies down on the blanket. I take off my glasses and undo my pony-tail, and then I snuggle in beside him. I pull the blanket over us. He nuzzles into my side and is asleep before I close my eyes.

I used to hate it when Elliot came into bed with me, because he gives off so much heat. Now I'm glad. He keeps me warm. I look after him. We're a team.

We'll be okay.

Chapter Fifteen

I'm freezing and my back is killing me. I open my eyes. I sit up and blink. For a second, I have no idea where I am—then the tree comes into focus, the red blanket, Elliot's Superman suit. I know where I am—and I don't like it.

I flop back down on the ground. My whole body is pounding.

What have I done?

The wind blows, and pine needles sprinkle down on us. I smell Colin again, and I have to open my eyes really, really wide to keep the tears from coming.

"Dad," I whisper.

I don't know if he's here or not, but just saying his name helps. I picture him, his arm around me. He'd do that. He'd comfort me.

At first. Then he'd tell me to get on with it. "When the going gets tough, the tough get going."

I don't move. I'm not sure how tough I am.

"Fake it until you make it." He also used to say that.

Right. What choice do I have?

I put on my glasses. I part the branches and look outside. No one's around. My guess is it's about 7:00 AM.

Breakfast time. I remember passing a convenience store on the way here. I hope it's open. I'm suddenly starving.

I give Elliot a shake, but he just puts his thumb in his mouth and rolls over. The poor kid is beat.

I'm going to let him sleep. We've got a big day ahead of us.

I ease my wallet out of our "pillow."

I check to make sure no one's around, and then I bolt out from under the tree. I've got to move fast. If Elliot wakes up while I'm gone, he'll totally freak out.

An older lady is just opening the store when I arrive. I pick up the big bundle of newspapers for her and carry them inside. I'm trying to be nice so she won't get suspicious.

Why would she get suspicious? I'm just a kid picking up some stuff for breakfast. It's not that unusual. Relax.

I wander up and down the aisles. Elliot likes yogurt, but it's a dollar for one little tub. We can't afford it. I grab a loaf of whole-grain bread instead. It's almost three dollars, but at least it will last a while. I look for the smallest jar of peanut butter I can find—but even that's too expensive.

I'm starting to get frantic again.

I put the bread back.

I grab a small bottle of juice, a box of granola bars and two bananas. I do the math in my head. It's over six dollars. That only leaves four.

I'll worry about that later.

The lady is putting the newspapers in the display case when I go to pay.

She wipes her hands on her smock and steps behind the counter to key in my stuff.

That's when I notice a big color picture of Elliot and me splashed over the front page of the newspaper.

Missing Stockbroker's Children Disappear.

Chapter Sixteen

The lady doesn't recognize me, but she must realize something's up. There's sweat streaming down my forehead.

"Will there be anything else?" she says.

I nod and grab a newspaper. I hand her my money. She gives me the bag and $2.43 change.

I say thank you and walk slowly out the door. I don't want her to remember the redheaded girl who bolted from the store.

I run as soon as I'm out of sight and don't stop until the park. Elliot's still asleep. I sit down and open the newspaper.

There's Mom—"the estranged wife of disgraced stockbroker, Steven Patterson"—pleading for our return. There's a quote from the guy I left the LeSabre with. There's a cop saying we're "believed to have boarded a bus to Cypress."

No mention of the man at the Lost and Found who gave us the clothes. Did he just not want to rat us out? Or was he worried about getting in trouble for giving us stuff that wasn't ours?

Who knows?

At least no one will be looking for a kid in a Superman suit yet. I've got to look on the bright side.

In the picture, I'm wearing my contacts. People probably won't recognize me in my glasses. My hair is longer now, but it's still red.

I'll cover it with my hood.

I turn the page.

Steve Patterson, former darling of the stock market, is suspected of defrauding his clients of hundreds of millions of dollars. With his company now worthless, it's highly unlikely any of his victims will ever be compensated. "Suicide is too good for that man," says Dave MacPherson, who admits that he will soon have to file for bankruptcy as a result of having invested all his savings with Patterson. "He wasn't just my financial advisor. He was my friend. And he ruined us."

I shove the newspaper into the garbage can where it belongs—then I slip under the branches to wake Elliot up.

Chapter Seventeen

Elliot is confused. He doesn't know why he has to pee outside or why he can't just sit down and eat his granola bar. Luckily, he's learned not to complain.

I grab my purse, stuff the blanket into the grocery bag and get going.

We have to get out of Cypress—the farther out, the better. I walk as fast as

I can—or rather as fast as *Elliot* can. It doesn't take me long to realize we have to do better than this.

I see a white-haired lady coming toward us. "Excuse me," I say.

She looks up and smiles.

"I lost my wallet, and my little brother's late for his doctor's appointment. I hate to ask—but would you mind lending us bus fare?"

Her smile fades a bit. I doubt she really believes me—but Elliot is pretty irresistible. She hands me five dollars.

I thank her. I wait until she's out of sight before I try the same trick on someone else. We'll use some of the money for bus fare, some for food.

It doesn't take long to collect twenty-three bucks. We could get more, but I don't want to be greedy. I'm also worried by how much Elliot has started to enjoy this. He coughs every time I mention his doctor's appointment.

The term *scam artist* jabs at my brain, but I ignore it. We're only doing this because we have to.

I'm holding Elliot's hand, waiting to cross the street, when a cop car drives by.

Are they looking for us? We can't wait around to find out. I drag Elliot across the street and make him keep running until we get to a field. I hear the sound of another car approaching. I pull Elliot down behind some bushes.

"Isn't this fun?" I say.

He's confused. "Sort of…," he says. He's trying so hard to be good.

Two cop cars speed by the other way.

"Want to wrestle?" I say and push Elliot down. He struggles, but I hold him there until I'm sure the cops are gone.

He comes up with such shock in his eyes. "You cheated!" he says. "You didn't wait until I was ready."

"You're right. That isn't fair," I say. *Nothing's fair*. I keep that part to myself.

Those cops are looking for us. I'm sure of it. It won't be safe to take another bus. I've got to figure something else out now.

I look around. There's a billboard on the edge of the field. It says, *This way to Camp Bonaventure: Where children's dreams come true!* A smaller sign below reads, *Closed for the season.*

I hear Dad's voice. *See? Something always comes up!*

A big black arrow points down the next road. How far could the camp be? We could hide out there for a while. We might not even have to hide very long. They only looked for Dad for five days. Why would they look longer for us?

"Hey, Elliot," I say. "How'd you like to go to a place where children's dreams come true?"

Chapter Eighteen

We cut across the field to the Camp Bonaventure road. I try to get Elliot singing songs that I remember from my own days at camp, but he's not going for it. He'll walk—but he's not happy.

He's even less happy when it starts to rain. Before long it's pouring, and the dirt road has turned to mud. There are too many hills to climb and nothing to take our minds off them. The only sights on the road are a few shabby houses tucked into the woods. My camp songs aren't cutting it anymore.

One of the houses has a satellite dish. Elliot says, "I want to stay with these people."

I wipe the water off my face and say, "No, I know a better place."

Elliot says, "Yeah, right," and laughs in a surprisingly adult way.

I hear a car engine rev. Elliot's face lights up as if someone's finally coming to rescue us, but I yank him into the woods before we're seen. We land in a little gully, and my shoes fill up with water. The car pulls out of a driveway and heads back in the direction of town.

Elliot starts sobbing. I hand him a banana as if it's the best treat in the world, then get him back on the road. We walk past the driveway where the car came out.

There's an old bike left on the lawn.

I don't even think about what I'm doing. I just grab the bike, sit Elliot on the crossbar and start pedaling.

"Did you just steal this bike?" he says. He's not crying anymore. In fact, he looks sort of delighted.

"Yes," I say. *Sometimes you just got to do what you got to do*. I don't know if Dad ever said that, but it wouldn't surprise me.

I pedal as hard as I can. I'm tired, but it makes me happy to see that Elliot is almost having fun.

It takes us about half an hour to get to Bonaventure. The driveway is barred by a metal gate. That's good, I think. We'll be safe here. We push the bike under the gate, then get back on and ride all the way down the hill to the camp. I make a big whooping sound as we splash through the puddles.

We come to a dead stop at the bottom of the hill. I do my best to sound positive, but it's hard to believe anyone's dreams ever came true here. The grass is brown. The lake is cold and gray. There's a playground, but the swings, the teeter-totter and the ball from the tetherball set are all missing. The buildings—the big wooden one in the middle and the little red cabins by the lake—are boarded up. Their paint is peeling.

Elliot slumps down on a rickety step with his fists on his cheeks. Rain streams down his face. "I don't like this camp," he says.

"You'll like it once we get inside!" My voice sounds fake even to me. I try all the doors and windows in the main hall. I yank away at the boards over each of the cabins. It's hopeless. Without a crowbar—and some biceps—I'm never going to get in.

I'm almost ready to give up when I notice another cabin tucked into the woods. It's got a sign out front that says

Cookie's Hideaway. I see right away that the door is open.

"Elliot!" I wave at him. "C'mon!"

The door isn't just open. It's right off its hinges. We run in out of the rain.

There are a bunch of empty beer cans on the floor. The chair is turned over, and books have been knocked off a little wooden shelf onto the single bed. It doesn't take me long to figure out what happened here. Some local kids obviously broke into the cabin to have themselves a party.

I silently thank them for their vandalism. They gave us a place to sleep.

I turn the chair over, tidy up the books, kick the beer cans under the bed. The cabin is cold and has a moldy smell, but it's better than another night outdoors. "There," I say. "Isn't this nice?"

Elliot tries to smile, but he's shivering. I can't let him get sick. I take our almost-dry clothes out of my purse, and we change. The mattress on the bed is damp, but it's softer than the floor. We snuggle up in the red blanket and share the last banana. We each have a granola bar for dessert. We play a game to see who can make it last the longest. Elliot only beats me because he hides a raisin in his hand. I take one tiny sip of juice, then let him have the rest. He's thirsty, and that's all he's had today.

We eventually warm up a bit. I'm feeling better about things again, but Elliot isn't. "I'm bored," he says.

I have to laugh. We've run away from home. Slept outside. Begged for money. Stolen a bike—and he's bored?

"Me too," I say. "Wanna play a game on my phone?"

I don't have to ask twice. Elliot's thrilled. Mom hardly ever lets him play video games.

I turn on my phone. I'm amazed there's coverage here at the end of the world.

My mailbox is full. I whip through the messages. I'm past the point of being disappointed that there's no word from Colin or even Helena—but I did sort of hope to hear from Sophie. I used to be able to count on her. Love sure ain't what it used to be.

(I guess I should have figured that out by now.)

Mom's the only one who tried to reach me. I hit *Delete*. I don't want to hear from her.

Elliot and I play Tetris for a while. I let him win every time, but he still doesn't last long. Even though it's barely dark out, he's ready for sleep. I turn off the phone, and we lie down on the lumpy mattress.

"I love you, Ria," he says.

"I love you too."

I've never meant anything more in my life. Some love is different.

Chapter Nineteen

I bolt up with a start. Someone's shaking me. It's so dark, I can't tell if my eyes are open or not. I'm not even sure I'm awake until I feel a sticky hand on my face and realize it's Elliot.

"I need my puffer, Ria." His breathing sounds like chalk squeaking across a blackboard.

I'm wide awake now. "Okay," I say in the most reassuring voice I can come up with. "Okay. Don't worry."

Why didn't I bring his puffer? He's used it three times a day for his entire life. What was I thinking?

I wasn't thinking. Or at least I wasn't thinking of *him*.

I get out of bed and stand in the doorway.

Relax, I tell myself. Elliot gets asthma attacks all the time. Lots of kids do. He hasn't died yet. He'll be fine.

How do I know that? This might be the one time he isn't.

What if something happened to Elliot? My heartbeats rattle off like machine-gun fire.

What do I do, Dad?

"Don't fret about your problems. Fix them."

I've got about twenty-five bucks. I'll go into town and buy him a puffer.

It's not that hard.

I look outside. It's dark and still pouring. I have no idea what time it is. It could be midnight, or it could be 4:00 AM.

I can't take Elliot. The rain will just make him worse.

I can't leave him here either. He'd be terrified.

And anyway, how much do puffers cost?

What if I need a prescription?

I'll have to find a doctor. I'll have to make up a fake name.

I turn and look back into the cabin. It's too dark to see Elliot, but I can hear him breathe. He sounds like a rocking chair with a squeaky joint.

I don't have a choice. I've got to call somebody for help.

Sophie.

Could I trust her?

I don't know. It's too dangerous.

That thing—the Kid's Helpline. It just pops into my head. I remember the commercial. They don't make you give your name. They'll know what to do.

I fumble back across the room. I stub my toe hard against the bed, but don't swear. I deserve the pain. I crawl onto the mattress and rub my hands over the blanket. I find my phone hidden under my purse and turn it on.

The screen lights up: 5:40 AM. Well, there's one question answered. It won't be long before daybreak.

I've got ten more messages. Six are from Mom. Three are from "Private Caller."

One is from Dad.

Chapter Twenty

"Honey," he says, "I'm so worried about you. Call me."

I can't believe my ears. I jump up, screaming, shaking.

Is this for real? Am I hallucinating?

I need proof. I replay the message. "Elliot," I say. "Who's that on the phone? Who is it?"

"Daddy! It's Daddy!" Even his asthma can't stop him from bouncing.

I check the date of the message. Last night. Just before midnight.

Is this a trick? Did some technical genius at the police department rig this up to fool us into calling?

I don't care. I dial the number.

Dad picks up on the first ring. "Ria?"

My hand slaps over my mouth. I can't answer for the longest time. "Is that you, Dad?"

Dad laughs. "Yes, it's me, honey."

"But...but..." I'm suddenly overcome by sobbing. "I thought you were dead. They said you were dead."

"Calm down, sweetie. It's a long story. I'll explain it all later. It's you we're worried about now. You and Elliot. Your mother says he needs his medicine."

I try to pull myself together. "He does. Please help me."

124

"Don't worry. We will. Tell me where you are. Someone will come and get you, right away."

"I want *you* to come, Dad," I say. "I want *you* to do it, Daddy."

I sound like a baby, but I don't care. I have to see him. I won't believe this isn't a trick or a hoax or just my wild imagination until I actually see him again.

He's talking to someone. I can't hear what he's saying. Is my mother there? Maybe they're back together. Maybe she was so happy to find out he's alive that they're back together again.

My old life. My family. My house. Maybe this was all just some big misunderstanding, and everything will be okay again. Mom and Dad and Elliot and me.

And Colin.

"I'm coming for you, Ria," Dad says. "Just tell me where you are."

It's only about an hour before we hear the first *thwack-thwack-thwack* overhead. Elliot and I run to the cabin door. The rain has stopped. The first glint of sun hits the blue and white police helicopter like a spotlight. Only Dad could have arranged that. It makes me think of an angel coming down from the clouds.

Elliot looks at me, confused. "Why are you crying, Ria? It's Daddy!" He says something else, but I can't make it out. The sound of the helicopter landing in the playground is deafening.

A policeman jumps out and races over to get us. We crouch down and run under the blades with him. I can see Dad sitting in the helicopter with that big beautiful smile of his. I'm so happy to see him.

I jump on board and throw my arms out to hug him. Last time I saw him, he hugged me so hard he made my bones squeak. This time, he doesn't even hug me back.

I'm surprised and hurt—until I pull back and see the handcuffs.

Chapter Twenty-One

I'm not very good at this. I got more strawberry jam on my uniform than in the donuts. I'm going to be sticky for the whole rest of my shift.

I'm standing by the sink, scrubbing at the bright red stain with a wet paper napkin when someone says, "Excuse me?"

I turn around and see Colin for the first time since I came back five months ago.

We're both embarrassed. He clearly wasn't expecting to see me here any more than I was expecting to see him.

I push my hairnet up off my fore-head. He takes a step back from the counter and says, "Sorry. I just wanted a blueberry muffin."

I nod about seven times. "We have blueberry muffins," I say. I grab a napkin and turn my back to him. I have to lean against the donut trays to keep my balance.

I realize he's wearing a uniform too. He must be working as a courier. I guess he has to. I heard his parents lost their house and their business and everything.

He must hate me.

I reach for the biggest muffin there is. As if that's going to make it up to him. He used to be so excited about going away to university this year, and now he's stuck here, having to work.

My hand is shaking so much I drop the muffin on the floor.

He says, "That's okay."

I shake my head. I put the muffin in the garbage and get another one.

Does he realize I didn't know anything about it? That my mother didn't know anything about it either until it was too late?

None of us had any idea Dad was capable of doing things like that. Stealing money. Scamming friends and relatives and helpless old ladies. Faking his own death. Taking off.

"Do you want it heated up?" I say. I'm so ashamed. I can't even look at Colin.

"No, it's good like that. Thanks."

"Butter?" I suddenly want him to stay. His voice doesn't sound angry at all. Maybe we could talk. I could explain everything to him.

What am I thinking? I couldn't explain anything to him. I don't *understand* anything. Part of me knows my father is a bad man. But another part of me still loves him, still even believes him, despite all the evidence against him.

And what difference does the evidence make any way? Dad may have done all those terrible things, but he turned himself in when he heard Elliot and I were missing, when he thought he could help get us back.

That must be worth something.

I just don't know how much.

Colin says, "No. No butter, thanks. I'm not playing hockey anymore, so I got to watch the calories."

He pats his perfectly flat stomach. I hand him the muffin in a little paper bag.

We're careful not to touch each other.

He puts five dollars on the counter.

"That's too much," I say. "It's only a dollar fifteen."

Colin shrugs. There's still a bit of sparkle in his eyes, even for me. "That's okay. Buy Elliot a treat."

He almost smiles. Then he walks out the door. I watch him disappear around the corner.

"Come back," I say—but I know by now he's too far gone.